JUST ME AND MY LITTLE BROTHER

BY
MERCER MAYER

For Arden and Benjamin
with love

A Random House PICTUREBACK® Book

Random House 🏠 New York

Just Me and My Little Brother book, characters, text, and images © 1991 Mercer Mayer. LITTLE CRITTER, MERCER MAYER'S LITTLE CRITTER, and MERCER MAYER'S LITTLE CRITTER and Logo are registered trademarks of Orchard House Licensing Company. All rights reserved. Published in the United States by Random House Children's Books, a division of Random House, Inc., New York. Originally published in 1991 by Golden Books Publishing Company, Inc. PICTUREBACK, RANDOM HOUSE, and the Random House colophon are registered trademarks of Random House, Inc.
www.randomhouse.com/kids
Educators and librarians, for a variety of teaching tools, visit us at
www.randomhouse.com/teachers
Library of Congress Control Number: 90-84584
ISBN-10: 0-307-12628-5   ISBN-13: 978-0-307-12628-3
Printed in the United States of America
16
· First Random House Edition 2006

We will do everything together,
just me and my little brother.
We will go to the orchard to pick apples,
and I will help him climb up.

We will have bunk beds,
and I will have the top
'cause I'm bigger.

We can play space wars.

We will be real tough,
just me and my little brother.

The bully will run away
when we come around.

We will stay up late and watch
the spooky shows on TV,
just me and my little brother.

At birthday parties we will eat
the most ice cream and cake,
just me and my little brother.

We can play cowboys and Indians,
and I'll let him catch me.

On Halloween we can go
trick-or-treating together,
just me and my little brother.

At Thanksgiving we will break
the wishbone, and I will let him win.

In the winter we will build a snowman.

We will build a snow fort
and have snowball fights.
Just me and my little brother
will be on the same side.

On Christmas morning
we will share our presents.

At Easter time we will hunt eggs together,
just me and my little brother.
And if he finds the most eggs,
I won't mind.

I will teach my little brother
to ride his bicycle.

He will have to practice a while.

There are so many
things we can do,
just me and my little brother.

Goo!

But first he'll have to
learn how to walk.